My First Illustrated B[ible]
Noah's Ark

Wonder House

So, he decided to wipe out all the life on Earth. Then, he saw Noah who was good and followed God's law.

'One day, while Noah was praying, God said to him, 'I have seen the goodness in you. Soon, I will send a great flood to destroy all the life on Earth. I will spare you and your family. Build an ark and get a pair of each species on it.'

Noah did exactly as God had commanded. The construction of the ark started immediately. Noah's three sons felled trees, cut logs and made them into planks. Noah put those pieces together to build an ark.

People laughed at him saying, 'Why build an ark? There is no sea for miles.' But Noah ignored them.

At last, the ark was complete. Soon, animals from all over the Earth came in pairs to the ark.

'Get inside the ark with your family,' God told Noah. He did so and shut the ark's door. Soon, the skies became darker and darker.

A drizzle started which soon became torrential rain. The rivers burst their banks and started to flood land. The ark started to rise. Frightened, people rushed to the hills and mountains.

It rained continuously for forty days and nights. All the life on Earth was destroyed. Only the ark remained afloat.

The rain stopped but the flood waters remained for months. Then, God sent a breeze and the water started to recede. Soon, the ark settled on Mount Ararat. Noah opened a window and let out a raven.

After sometime, the raven returned. Noah knew that the Earth was not dry yet. Days later, he let out a dove and it returned with an olive branch. Noah waited still.

Days later, Noah saw that the plants had started to grow. Once again, he let out a dove. It did not return. Then, he let out all the animals.

He built an altar for God to thank Him. God said, 'I promise that I will not destroy life on Earth again.'

Then, a rainbow appeared in the sky. 'This rainbow is the witness of my promise to you Noah and to all the generations of men and living creatures to come,' said God. Noah thanked the God and started life afresh.